Mouse Goes To The Beach

By Jimmy Danelli   Illustrated by Maureen Danelli

Mouse was happy to be at the beach.

The sand felt warm and soft on his little feet.

Goose took out the sunscreen and applied the lotion onto Mouse.

"What is that?" Mouse asked.

"It's to protect your skin from the sun," Goose replied.

Chipper turned to Mouse and said, "It's time to get our feet wet."

"Oh, goody!" Mouse exclaimed.

Mouse stood with Chipper and Goose in the cool ocean water.

"I like the beach!" said Mouse.

Suddenly, Chipper noticed something swimming in the ocean.

"Look! It's a whale!" he said.

Chipper lifted Mouse up onto his shoulders so he could see the whale.

"I see it! I see it!" Mouse said excitedly.

Later in the day, Mouse was building a sandcastle when he noticed a baby sea turtle trying to make his way to the ocean.

"Look! The baby turtle is trying to get to the water!" Mouse said.

"That's because sea turtles spend most of their lives in the ocean. However, many of them don't make it into the water like they used to," Chipper explained.

"How come?" Mouse wanted to know.

"Because of climate change, much of the sand has been replaced with rocks which get in the turtle's way," Goose said with a tear in her eye.

"Isn't there anything we can do to help?" Mouse asked.

Chipper thought for a moment.

"Well, if we put the turtle in your pail, you can carry him to the water," he said.

So, they did just that.

After the baby turtle was in the pail, Mouse carried him to the water where he let him go.

They watched as the baby turtle swam out to sea.

"Goodbye, baby turtle," Mouse said.

"Do you think the baby turtle will be alright?" Mouse asked.

"I think he'll be just fine," replied Goose.

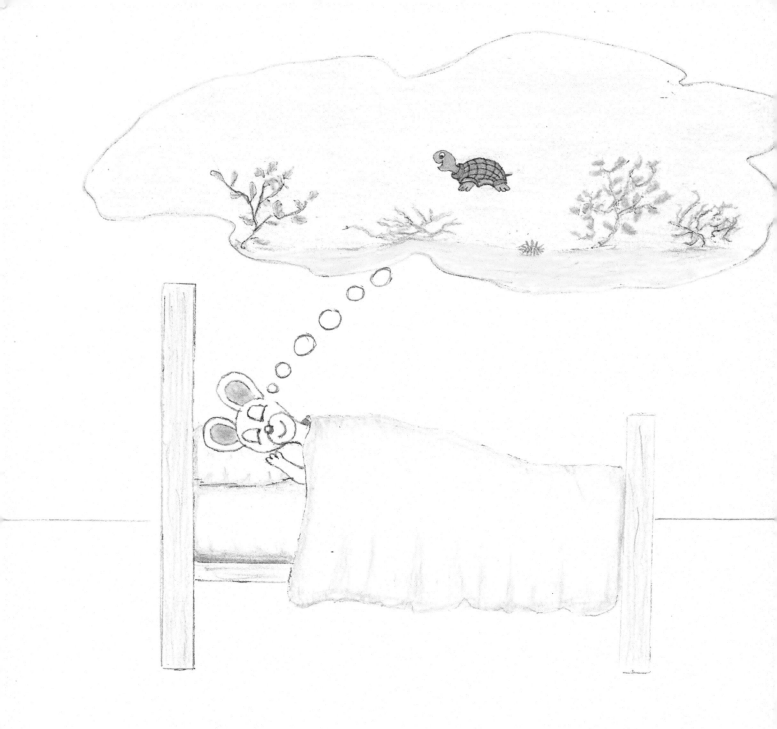

That night, as Mouse slept in his bed, he dreamed of the baby turtle.

CPSIA information can be obtained
at www.ICGtesting.com
Printed in the USA
LVOW05s2317251016
510286LV00015B/56/P